A-TRAIN ALLEN

LESLEY YOUNGE • Illustrated by LONNIE OLLIVIERRE

PUBLISHED by SLEEPING BEAR PRESS™

IT WAS THREE O'CLOCK IN THE AFTERNOON,
and everyone knew that A-TRAIN ALLEN
would soon come FLYING by.

A-Train lived on Holly Street,
which was not too far from his school.
In the mornings, he took his time. But after school, he **RAN**.
It was widely believed that he could
get across town faster than the subway.

When the final school bell rang, the neighbors and shopkeepers and old men playing chess in the park would check the time and say,

"GUESS A-TRAIN WILL BE ALONG SOON."

Shortly after, here he'd come, **BARRELING** through, his sneakers **FLAPPING** against the pavement,

his backpack **BOUNCING**, and a little gust of wind **WHOOSHING** by, because—

MAAAAN! THAT BOY WAS FAST.

This afternoon was no different.
After **BOUNDING** out the front door of his school,
A-Train **BOLTED** through the park.

He **FLEW** past a group of older kids playing basketball, who stopped their game to watch him go.

A flock of pigeons took to the air, and the lady feeding them smiled as she threw another handful of bread crumbs onto the ground.

The old men playing chess under the ginkgo trees laughed and remembered a time when they too could run like that.

Once he **BOLTED** through the park, A-Train **SPED** past the library.
The window display was a tempting blur of books.
A girl sat on the bench outside, reading.

The pages of her book
FLUTTERED
as A-Train passed.

After **SPEEDING** past the library,
he **DASHED** toward the post office,
arriving just as the mail trucks rolled out for afternoon delivery.
He **SKIDDED** to a stop at the curb and paused long enough
to let the last truck turn onto Center Street, where he was headed, too.

The driver gave a friendly honk.

A-Train **WAVED**
and took off again.

Center Street was **BUSTLING** as people gathered on corners and customers **SCURRIED** in and out of the various shops. A-Train **DUCKED** and **DODGED** his way down the sidewalk.

"A-TRAIN, A-TRAIN! WHERE YOU GOING SO FAST?"

the grocer called as she arranged piles of oranges and avocados.

"GOT SOMEWHERE TO BE, GOT SOMEWHERE TO BE," A-Train called back.

"A-TRAIN, A-TRAIN! WHERE YOU GOING SO FAST?" the barber hollered as he swept his doorway.

"GOT SOMEWHERE TO BE, GOT SOMEWHERE TO BE,"

A-Train hollered back.

"A-TRAIN, A-TRAIN! WHERE YOU GOING SO FAST?" the mustached man behind the hot dog stand shouted as he squeezed out some mustard.

"GOT SOMEWHERE TO BE, GOT SOMEWHERE TO BE,"

A-Train shouted back.

He didn't slow down until he reached the elevated subway station.

The tracks **TREMBLED** overhead as a train **RUMBLED** closer, bringing folks back home from the cluster of skyscrapers downtown.

The train **SCREECHED** to a stop.
He heard the doors **HISS** open.
The conductor's garbled voice warned
boarding passengers to stand back.

Moments later, A-Train's grandmother came down the stairs. When she reached the bottom, she stepped onto the sidewalk and adjusted her hat.

A-Train was right there to meet her.
"MADE IT ON TIME, GRANDMA,"
he said.

"YES, YOU DID, BABY. SEEMS LIKE YOU BEAT ME HERE EVERY SINGLE DAY. YOU SURE ARE FAST."

She gave him a squeeze around the shoulders and a kiss right on the top of his head.

A-Train smiled and took her hand.

To Grandma Ida & Grandma Dot; my father, who is my champion;

and Allen, who will always be the reason why.

—Lesley

To Nickola Montague for always believing in me. Thank you.

—Lonnie

SLEEPING BEAR PRESS™

2395 South Huron Parkway, Suite 200, Ann Arbor, MI 48104
www.sleepingbearpress.com
© Sleeping Bear Press
Printed and bound in China.

10 9 8 7 6 5 4 3 2 1

Library of Congress Cataloging-in-Publication Data
Names: Younge, Lesley, author. | Ollivierre, Lonnie, illustrator.
Title: A-train Allen / Lesley Younge ; illustrated by Lonnie Ollivierre.
Description: Ann Arbor, MI : Sleeping Bear Press, [2023] | Audience: Ages
4-8. | Summary: Allen, known as A-Train because he is the fastest kid
around, races through the city towards the one thing that will get him to slow down.
Identifiers: LCCN 2022037902 | ISBN 9781534111837 (hardcover)
Subjects: CYAC: Grandparent and child—Fiction. | Grandmothers—Fiction. |
African Americans—Fiction. | LCGFT: Picture books.
Classification: LCC PZ7.1.Y825 At 2023 | DDC [E]—dc23
LC record available at https://lccn.loc.gov/2022037902